THIS WALKER BOOK BELONGS TO:

_____

_____

_____

_____

"Hello, great big bullfrog!"

Colin West

WALKER BOOKS
AND SUBSIDIARIES
LONDON · BOSTON · SYDNEY · AUCKLAND

"Hello, I'm a great big bullfrog,"
said the great big bullfrog.

"Hello, great big bullfrog!
Guess who I am!"

"I'm a great big rat,"
  said the great big rat
  to the great big bullfrog.

"Hello, great big rat!
Guess who I am!"

"I'm a great big warthog,"
said the great big warthog
to the great big rat
and the great big bullfrog.

"Hello, great big warthog!
Guess who I am!"

"I'm a great big tiger,"
   said the great big tiger
   to the great big warthog
   and the great big rat
   and the great big bullfrog.

"Hello, great big tiger!
Guess who I am!"

"I'm a great big bear,"
said the great big bear
to the great big tiger
and the great big warthog
and the great big rat
and the great big bullfrog.

"Let's have
a great big
HULLABALOO!"

But the great big bullfrog
didn't want a great big hullabaloo.

He didn't feel
so great and
big any more.
He felt a tiddly
little bullfrog.

"Goodbye, everybody!"
said the not so great big bullfrog.

But suddenly...

"Hello, great
big bullfrog!
Guess who I am!"

"I'm a great big bumble bee,"
said the great big bumble bee.

"And I'm a great big bullfrog!"
said the great big bullfrog.
"A great

    great

        great big bullfrog!"

COLIN WEST knows that reading **"Hello, great big bullfrog!"** aloud can be great fun. He says, "The bullfrog could have a croaky voice, the rat a squeaky one and the bear a deep one, for instance. By the way, did you notice how the front endpapers are different from those at the back of the book?"

Colin West enjoys working on all types of book, including poetry and story books. He is the author/illustrator of many books, including the Giggle Club titles *Buzz, Buzz, Buzz, Went Bumble-bee*; *"I Don't Care!" Said the Bear*; *One Day in the Jungle* and *"Only Joking!" Laughed the Lobster* as well as the jungle tales *"Go tell it to the toucan!"*; *"Have you seen the crocodile?"*; *"Not me," said the monkey* and *"Pardon?" said the giraffe*. Colin lives in Epping, Essex.

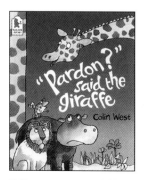

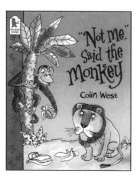

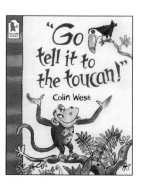

ISBN 0-7445-8257-1 (pb) ISBN 0-7445-8256-3 (pb) ISBN 0-7445-8254-7 (pb) ISBN 0-7445-8253-9 (pb)